TALKING TALES

YUMMM!!

Elijah, the boy and the amazing famine feast

Bob Hartman

Illustrations by Emma Hagan

CWR

For Micah

Copyright © Bob Hartman 2014

Published 2015 by CWR, Waverley Abbey House, Waverley Lane, Farnham, Surrey GU9 8EP, UK.

CWR is a Registered Charity – Number 294387 and a Limited Company registered in England – Registration Number 1990308.

The right of Bob Hartman to be identified as the author of this work has been asserted by him
in accordance with the Copyright, Designs and Patents Act 1988 sections 77 and 78.

Visit www.cwr.org.uk/distributors for a list of National Distributors.

Concept development, editing, design and production by CWR.

Illustrations by Emma Hagan, visit www.emmahagan.co.uk

Printed in the UK by Linney Group

ISBN: 978-1-78259-359-1

This story is found in
1 Kings 16:29—33 and 17:1—16

Sorry.

Don't mean to talk with my mouth full.
It's just that it's been a long time since
I've had anything to eat.

And these cakes are sooooo delicious.

Think I'll have
another one.

The people at the table ...?

Well, the lady is my mum.
And the guy? He's sort of the
reason we have these cakes.
And, weirdly, also sort of
the reason we were starving in
the first place. It's a long story.

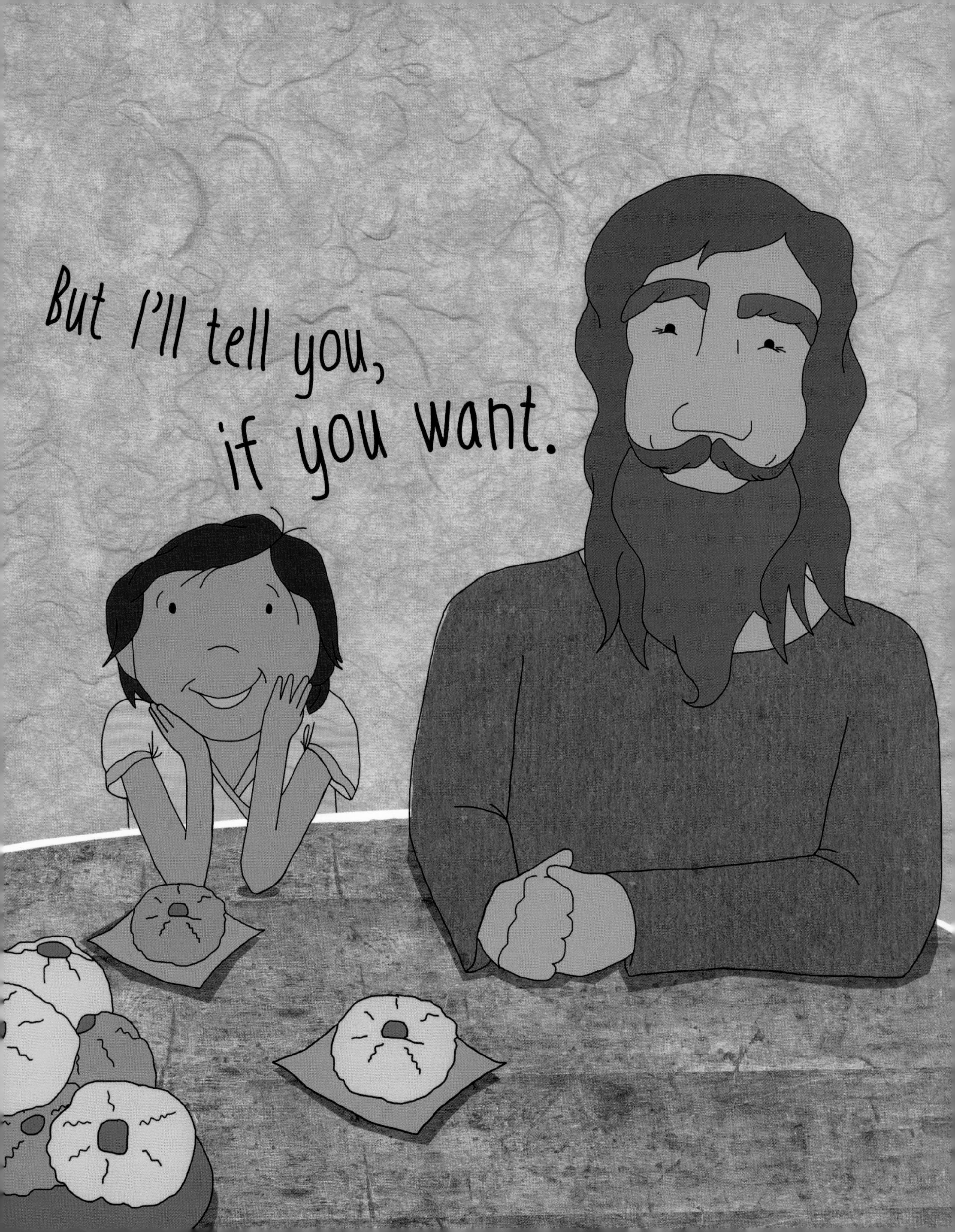
But I'll tell you,
if you want.

And he's an Israelite.
So he's not from round here, in Sidon.

And he's also a prophet of the God of Israel,
which means God talks to him
and tells him stuff.

And that's sort of where the story starts.

You see, according to Elijah, God was angry with Israel's king, Ahab, so He told him that unless he changed his evil ways, the rain would

s
t
o
p

f
a
l
l
i
n
g.

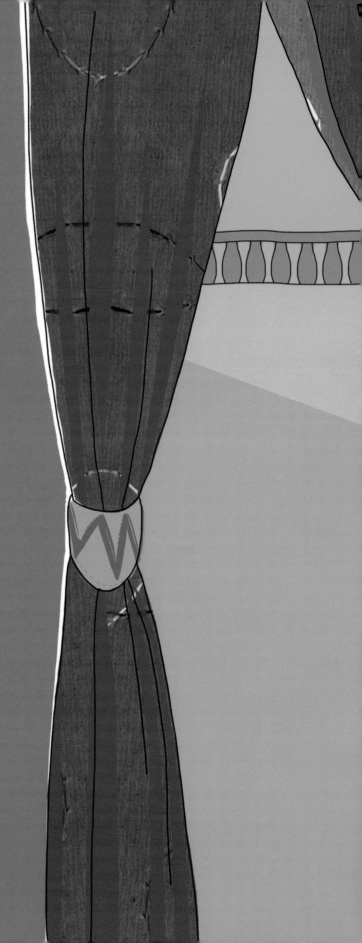

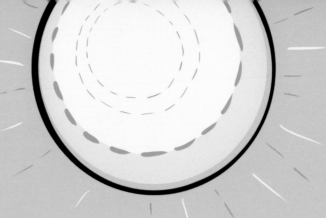

Ahab didn't change.

The rain stopped falling.

The crops stopped growing.

And because Israel is next door to Sidon,

all that happened to us, too.

Nice one, I know.

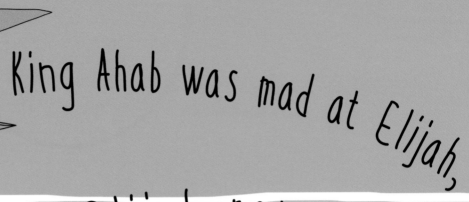

King Ahab was mad at Elijah,

so Elijah ran away.

He hid in this valley where he drank from a little, tiny stream. And, get this, he says that ravens brought him his dinner every day.

Yeah, I found it kind of hard to believe, too.

But Elijah swears it's true.

'Rawk! What will we be having today, sir?'

'Rawk! Shall I take the drinks order first?'

'Rawk! Would you like beans with that?'

Eventually, the stream dried up, so God sent him here, to Sidon.

And that's where me and my mum
come into the story.
She was out by the city gates,
collecting wood to make a fire ...

Elijah came up to her and asked her for some water and some bread.

She couldn't believe it. She tried to explain to him that all she had left was some oil in a jug and a little flour in a jar.

She told him that she was going to make some bread out of it. Then we were going to eat it. Then we were going to starve.

Honestly, it was as bad as that.

But Elijah didn't seem worried at all.
He told my mum not to be afraid.

He told her to bake him a cake
– before she even baked **anything for us!**

And then he told her the strangest thing of all.

He told her if she did that, then the oil in the jug

and the flour in the jar would not run out until it started raining again.

It was God's promise, he said, and she could count on it.

So my mum did what Elijah's God told her to do.

What happened?

See that pile of cakes over there?
That's what happened! And no matter how many
she makes, there's always oil and flour to make more.

So Elijah's staying
for a bit.

We're not starving,
which is a big improvement.
Life's a lot better,
all in all.

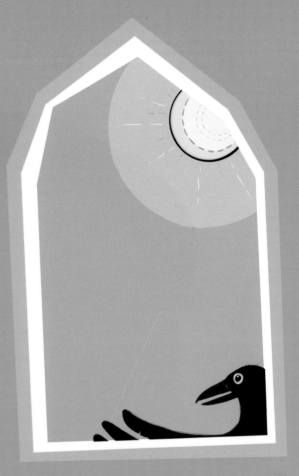

Except for one thing ...

I tell Elijah and he just laughs.

Rawk

Look out for another Talking Tale ...
SHHHH!! — Miriam, the baby and the secret basket boat